John Dryden

King Arthur

The British worthy

John Dryden

King Arthur
The British worthy

ISBN/EAN: 9783742842220

Manufactured in Europe, USA, Canada, Australia, Japa

Cover: Foto ©Andreas Hilbeck / pixelio.de

Manufactured and distributed by brebook publishing software
(www.brebook.com)

John Dryden

King Arthur

King ARTHUR:

OR,

The British Worthy.

A *Dramatick*

OPERA.

Perform'd at the *QUEENS* Theatre
by Their MAJESTIES Servants.

Written by Mr. DRYDEN.

—————— *H.ic alta Theatris*
Fundamenta locant: Scenis decora alta futuris. Virg. Æneid.
Purpurea intexti tollunt aulæa Britanni. Georg. 3. 10.
——————*Tanton' placuit concurrere motu.* Æneid. 1.
Jupiter, æternâ Genteis in pace futuras?
Et Celebrare Domeſtica faſta. Hor.

ration (the inherent Virtues of His Family) be re-
membred with a Grateful Veneration by Three King-
doms, through which He fpread the Bleffings of them.
And, as your Lordfhip held a principal *Place* in His
Efteem, and perhaps the firft in His Affection, during
His latter Troubles ; the Succefs which accompanied
thofe prudent Counfels, cannot but reflect an Honour
on thofe few who manag'd them; and wrought out,
by their Faithfulnefs and Diligence, the *Publick* Safety. I might dilate on the Difficulties which attended
that Undertaking, the Temper of the *People*, the
Power, Arts and Intereft of the contrary *Party*, but
thofe are all of them Invidious Topicks ; they are too
green in our Remembrance ; and he who touches on
them, *Incedit per ignes, fuppofitos cineri dolofo.* But
without reproaching one fide to praife another, I
may juftly recommend to both, thofe wholfom Counfels, which wifely adminiftred, and as well executed,
were the Means of preventing a Civil War, and of
extinguifhing a growing Fire which was juft ready to
have broken forth among us. So many Wives, who
have yet their Husbands in their Arms ; fo many *Pa*-
rents, who have not the Number of their Children
leffen'd ; fo many Villages, Towns and Cities, whofe
Inhabitants are not decreas'd, their *Property* violated,
or their Wealth diminifh'd, are yet owing to the fober
Conduct, and happy Refults of your Advice. If a
true Account may be expected by future Ages, from
the prefent, your Lordfhip will be delivered over to
Pofterity, in a fairer Character than I have given :
And be read, not in the *Preface* of a *Play*, (whofe
Author is not vain enough to promife Immortality to
others

others, or to hope it for himself) but in many Pages of a Chronicle, fill'd with Praises of your Administration. For if Writers be just to the Memory of King *CHARLES* the Second, they cannot deny him to have been an exact Knower of Mankind, and a perfect Distinguisher of their Talents. 'Tis true, his Necessities often forc'd him to vary his Councellours and Councils, and sometimes to employ such Persons in the Management of his Affairs, who were rather fit for his present purpose, than satisfactory to his Judgment: But where it was Choice in him, not Compulsion, he was Master of too much good Sense to delight in heavy Conversation; and whatever his Favourites of State might be, yet those of his Affection, were Men of Wit. He was easie with these; and comply'd only with the former: But in the latter part of his Life, which certainly requir'd to be most cautiously manag'd, his secret Thoughts were communicated but to few; and those selected of that sort, who were *Amici omnium Horarum*, able to advise him in a serious Consult, where his *Honour* and Safety were concern'd; and afterwards capable of entertaining him with pleasant Discourse, as well as profitable. In this Maturest part of his Age, when he had been long season'd with Difficulties and Dangers, and was grown to a Niceness in his Choice, as being satisfied how few cou'd be trusted; and, of those who cou'd be trusted, how few cou'd serve him, he confined himself to a small Number of Bosom Friends; amongst whom, the World is much mistaken, if your Lordship was not first.

It

If the Rewards which you receiv'd for thoſe Services, were only *Honours*, it rather ſhew'd the Neceſſities of the Times, than any want of Kindneſs in your Royal Maſter: And as the Splendour of your Fortune ſtood not in need of being ſupported by the Crown, ſo likewiſe in being ſatisfied without other Recompence, you ſhow'd your ſelf to be above a Mercenary Intereſt; and ſtrengthen'd that Power, which beſtowed thoſe Titles on you: Which truly ſpeaking, were Marks of Acknowledgment more than Favour.

But, as a Skilful Pilot will not be tempted out to Sea, in ſuſpected Weather, ſo have you wiſely choſen to withdraw your ſelf from publick Buſineſs, when the Face of *Heaven* grew troubled; and the frequent ſhifting of the Winds foreſhew'd a Storm: There are Times and Seaſons when the beſt Patriots are willing to withdraw their *Hands* from the Commonwealth; as *Phocion* in his latter Days was obſerv'd to decline the Management of Affairs: Or, as *Cicero*, (to draw the Similitude more home) left the Pulpit, for *Tuſculum*, and the praiſe of Oratory, for the ſweet Enjoyments of a private Life. And, in the Happineſs of thoſe Retirements, has more oblig'd Poſterity by his *Moral Precepts*, than he did the Republick, in quelling the Conſpiracy of *Catiline.* What prudent Man, wou'd not rather follow the Example of his Retreat, than ſtay like *Cato*, with a ſtubborn unſeaſonable Virtue, to oppoſe the Torrent of the People, and at laſt be driven from the Market-place by a Riot of a Multitude, uncapable of Counſel, and deaf to Eloquence? There is likewiſe a Portion of our Lives, which every

Wife Man may juftly referve to his own peculiar ufe, and that without defrauding his Native Coutry. A Roman Soldier was allow'd to plead the Merit of his Services for his difmiffion at fuch an Age; and there was but one Exception to that Rule, which was, an Invafion from the *Gauls.* How far that, may work with your Lordfhip, I am not certain; but I hope it is not coming to the Trial.

In the mean time, while the Nation is fecur'd from Foreign Attempts, by fo powerful a Fleet, and we enjoy not only the Happinefs, but even the Ornaments of Peace, in the Divertifement of the Town, I humbly offer you this Trifle, which if it fucceed upon the Stage, is like to be the chiefeft Entertainment of our Ladies and Gentlemen this Summer. When I wrote it, feven Years ago, I employ'd fome reading about it, to inform my felf out of *Beda, Bochartus,* and other Authors, concerning the Rites and Cuftoms of the Heathen Saxons; as I alfo us'd the little Skill I have in Poetry to adorn it. But not to offend the prefent Times, nor a Government which has hitherto protected me, I have been oblig'd fo much to alter the firft Defign, and take away fo many Beauties from the Writing, that it is now no more what it was formerly, than the prefent Ship of the *Royal Sovereign,* after fo often taking down, and altering, to the Veffel it was at the firft Building. There is nothing better, than what I intended, but the Mufick; which has fince arriv'd to a greater Perfction in *England,* than ever formerly; efpecially paffing through the Artful Hands of Mr. *Purcel,* who has

Com-

Compos'd it with fo great a Genius, that he has nothing to fear but an ignorant, ill-judging Audience. But the Numbers of Poetry and Vocal Mufick, are fometimes fo contrary, that in many places I have been oblig'd to cramp my Verfes, and make them rugged to the Reader, that they may be harmonious to the Hearer: Of which I have no Reafon to repent me, becaufe thefe forts of Entertainment are principally defign'd for the Ear and Eye ; and therefore in Reafon my Art on this occafion, ought to be fubfervient to his And befides, I flatter my felf with an Imagination, that a Judicious Audience will eafily diftinguifh betwixt the Songs, wherein I have comply'd with him, and thofe in which I have followed the Rules of Poetry, in the Sound and Cadence of the Words Notwithftanding all thefe Difadvantages, there is fomewhat ftill remaining of the firft Spirit with which I wrote it : And, though I can only fpeak by ghefs, of what pleas'd my firft and beft Patronefs the Dutchefs of *Monmouth* in the reading, yet I will venture my Opinion, by the knowledge I have long had of her Graces Excellent Judgment, and true tafte of Poetry, that the parts of the Airy and Earthy Spirits, and that Fairy kind of writing, which depends only upon the Force of Imagination, were the Grounds of her liking the Poem, and afterwards of her Recommending it to the Queen I have likewife had the fatisfaction to hear, that *Her* Majefty has Gracioufly been pleas'd to perufe the Manufcript of this *Opera*, and given it *Her* Royal Approbation Poets, who fubfift not but on the Favour of Sovereign Princes, and of great Perfons,

may

may have leave to be a little vain, and boaſt of their Patronage, who encourage the Genius that animates them. And therefore *I* will again preſume to gheſs, that *Her* Majeſty was not diſpleas'd to find in this Poem the *Praiſes* of *Her* Native Country; and the Heroick Actions of ſo famous a *Predeceſſor* in the Government of *Great Britain*, as King *Arthur*.

All this, My Lord, *I* muſt confeſs, looks with a kind of Inſinuation, that *I* preſent you with ſomewhat not unworthy your *Protection* : But *I* may eaſily miſtake the Favour of *Her* Majeſty for *Her* Judgment :: *I* think *I* cannot be deceiv'd in thus addreſſing to your Lordſhip, whom *I* have had the Honour to know, at that diſtance which becomes me, for ſo many Years. 'Tis true, that formerly *I* have ſhadow'd ſome part of your Virtues, under another Name ; but the Character, though ſhort and imperfect, was ſo true, that it broke through the Fable, and was diſcover'd by its Native Light. What *I* pretend by this Dedication, is an Honour which *I* do my ſelf to *Poſterity*, by acquainting them that *I* have been converſant with the firſt *Perſons* of the Age in which *I* liv'd; and thereby perpetuate my *Proſe*, when my Verſes may poſſibly be forgotten, or obſcur'd by the Fame of Future *Poets*. Which Ambition, amongſt my other Faults and Imperfections, be pleaſed to pardon, in

My LORD,

Your Lordſhips moſt Obedient Servant,

John Dryden.

Dramatis Personæ.

King *Arthur.* ——————— Mr. *Betterton*
　Ofwald, King of *Kent*, a Saxon ⎰Mr. *Willia*
　and a Heathen. ——————— ⎱
Conon, Duke of *Cornwal*, Tributary ⎰Mr. *Hodgfo*
　to King *Arthur.* ⎱
Merlin, a famous Inchanter. ———Mr. *Kynafto*
Ofmond, a Saxon Magician, and a ⎰Mr. *Sandfo*
　Heathen. ——— ——————— ⎱
Aurelius, Friend to *Arthur.* ———— Mr. *Alexand*
Albanact, Captain of *Arthur*'s Guards.–Mr. *Bowen.*
Guillamar, Friend to *Ofwald.* ——— Mr. *Harris.*

W O M E N.

Emmeline, Daughter of *Conon.* ——–Mrs. *Bracegi*
Matilda, her Attendant. ————–Mrs. *Richar*

Philidel, an Airy Spirit. ———–——Mrs. *Butler.*
Grimbald, an Earthy Spirit.———— Mr. *Bowman*

Officers and Soldiers, Singers and Dancers, &

Scene in *K E N T.*

King

Prologue to the OPERA,

Spoken by Mr. *Betterton*.

SUre there's a Dearth of Wit in this dull Town,
  When silly Plays so savourly go down :
As when Clipp'd Money passes, 'tis a sign
A Nation is not over-stock'd with Coin.
Happy is he, who, in his own Defence,
Can Write just level to your humble Sence ;
Who higher than your Pitch can never go ;
And doubtless, he must creep, who Writes below.
So have I seen in Hall of Knight, or Lord,
A weak Arm, throw on a long Shovel-Board,
He barely lays his Piece, bar Rubs and Knocks,
Secur'd by Weakness not to reach the Box.
A Feeble Poet will his Bus'ness do ;
Who straining all he can, comes up to you :
For if you like your Selves, you like him too.
An Ape his own Dear Image will embrace ;
An ugly Beau adores a Hatchet Face :
So some of you, on pure instinct of Nature,
Are led, by Kind, t' admire your fellow Creature.
In fear of which, our House has sent this Day,
T' insure our New-Built-Vessel, call'd a Play.
No sooner Nam'd, than one crys out, These Stagers
Come in good time, to make more Work for Wagers.
The Town divides, if it will take, or no ;
The Courtiers Bet, the Cits, the Merchants too ;
A sign they have but little else to do.

                                  Betts,

Betts, at the first, were *Fool-Traps* ; where the *Wise*
Like *Spiders*, lay in *Ambush* for the *Flies* :
But now they're grown a common Trade for all,
And Actions, by the News-Book, Rise and Fall.
Wits, *Cheats*, and *Fops*, are free of *VVager-Hall*.
One Policy, as far as Lyons carries ;
Another, nearer home sets up for Paris.
Our *Betts*, at last, wou'd ev'n to Rome extend,
But that the *Pope* has prov'd our Trusty Friend.
Indeed, it were a *Bargain*, worth our *Money*,
Cou'd we insure another Ottobuoni.
Among the rest, there are a sharping Sett,
That Pray for us, and yet against us Bett :
Sure Heav'n it self, is at a loss to know,
If these wou'd have their Pray'rs be heard, or no :
For in great Stakes, we piously suppose,
Men Pray but very faintly they may lose.
Leave off these *VVagers* ; for in Conscience Speaking,
The City needs not your new *Tricks* for *Breaking* :
nd if you Gallants lose, to all appearing
'll want an Equipage for Volunteering ;
k thus, no Spark of Honour left within ye,
you shou'd draw the Sword, you draw the Quidam.

King ARTHUR:

OR,

The Britiſh Worthy.

ACT I. SCENE I.

Enter Conon, Aurelius, Albanact.

Con. THen this is the deciding Day, to fix
Great *Britain*'s Scepter in great *Arthur*'s Hand.
   Aur. Or put it in the bold Invaders gripe.
   Arthur and *Oſwald*, and their different Fates,
Are weighing now within the Scales of Heaven.
  Con. In Ten ſet Battles have we driven back
Theſe Heathen Saxons, and regain'd our Earth.
As Earth recovers from an Ebbing Tide,
Her half-drown'd Face, and lifts it o'er the Waves.
From *Severn*'s Banks, even to this *Barren-Down*,
Our foremoſt Men have preſt their fainty Rear,
And not one Saxon Face has been beheld ;
But all their Backs, and Shoulders have been ſtuck
With foul diſhoneſt Wounds : Now here, indeed,
Becauſe they have no further Ground, they ſtand.
  Aur. Well have we choſe a Happy day for Fight ;
For every Man, in courſe of time, has found
Some days are lucky, ſome unfortunate.

B

A'b.

Alb. But why this day more lucky than the reſt?

Con. Becauſe this day
Is Sacred to the Patron of our Iſle;
A Chriſtian, and a Souldiers Annual Feaſt.   (*doria's* Day.

Alb. Oh, now I underſtand you, This is St. *George* of *Cappa-*
Well, It may be ſo, but Faith I was Ignorant; we Soldiers
Seldom examine the Rubrick; and now and then a Saint may
Happen to ſlip by us; But if he be a Gentleman Saint, he will
Forgive us.

Con. Oſwald, undoubtedly will Fight it bravely.

Aur. And it behoves him well, 'tis his laſt Stake. [*To* Alb.
But what manner of Man is this *Oſwald?* Have ye ever ſeen him?

Al. Ne'er but once; & that was to my Coſt too; I follow'd him
And to ſay Truth, ſomwhat Uncivilly, upon a Rout; (too cloſe,
But he turn'd upon me, as quick and as round, as a chaff'd Boar;
And gave me two Licks acroſs the Face, to put me
In mind of my Chriſtianity.

Con. I know him well; he's free and open Hearted.

Aur. His Countries Character: That Speaks a German.

Con. Revengeful, rugged, violently brave; and once re-
ſolv'd is never to be mov'd.

Alb. Yes, he's a valiant Dog, Pox on him.

Con. This was the Character he then maintain'd,
When in my Court, he ſought my Daughters Love:
My Fair, Blind, *Emmeline.*   (wall:

Alb. I cannot blame him for Courting the Heireſs of *Corn-*
All Heireſſes are Beautiful; and as Blind as ſhe is, he would have
No Blind Bargain of her.   (had.

Aur. For that Defeat in Love, he rais'd this War.
For Royal *Arthur* Reign'd within her Heart,
Ere *Oſwald* mov'd his Sute.

Con. Ay, now *Aurelius,* you have Nam'd a Man;
One, whom beſides the Homage that I owe,
As *Cornwall's* Duke, to his Imperial Crown,
I wou'd have choſen out, from all Mankind,
To be my Soveraign Lord.

Aur. His Worth divides him from the crowd of Kings;
So Born, without Deſert to be ſo Born;
Men, ſet aloft, to be the Scourge of Heaven;
And with long Arms, to laſh the Under-World.

                                             Con.

Con. Arthur is all that's Excellent in *Oswald*;
And void of all his Faults : In Battle brave ;
But still Serene in all the Stormy War,
Like Heaven above the Clouds; and after Fight,
As Merciful and Kind, to vanquisht Foes,
As a Forgiving God ; but see, he's here,
And Praise is Dumb before him.

Enter King Arthur, *Reading a Letter, with Attendants.*

Arthur ⎧Go on, Auspicious Prince, the Stars are kind :
Reading.⎩Unfold thy Banners to the willing Wind ;
While I, with Aiery Legions, help thy Arms ;
Confronting Art with Art, and Charms with Charms.
So *Merlin* writes; nor can we doubt th' event,   [*To* Con.
With Heav'n and you to Friends ; Oh Noble *Conon*,
You taught my tender Hands the Trade of War ;
And now again you Helm your hoary Head,
And under double weight of Age and Arms,
Affert your Countries Freedom, and my Crown.
  Con. No more, my Son.
  Arth. Most happy in that Name !
Your *Emmeline*, to *Oswald's* Vows refus'd,
You made my plighted Bride :
Your Charming Daughter, who like Love, Born Blind,
Un-aiming hits, with surest Archery,
And Innocently kills.
  Con. Remember, Son,
You are a General, other Wars require you.
For see the *Saxon* Grofs begins to move.
  Arth. Their Infantry Embattel'd, square and close;
March firmly on, to fill the middle Space:
Cover'd by their advancing Cavalry.
By Heav'n, 'tis Beauteous Horrour :
The Noble *Oswald* has provok'd my Envy.

Enter Emmeline, *led by* Matilda.

Ha ! Now my Beauteous *Emmeline* appears
Anew, but Oh, a softer Flame, inspires me :
          Even

Even Rage and Vengeance, flumber at her fight.

Con. Hafte your Farewel; I'll chear my Troops, and wait ye.

           [*Exit* Conon.

Em. Oh Father, Father, I am fure you're here;
Becaufe I fee your Voice.

Arth. No, thou miftak'ft thy hearing for thy fight;
He's gone, my *Emmeline*;
And I but ftay to gaze on thofe fair Eyes,
Which cannot view the Conqueft they have made.
Oh Star-like Night, dark only to thy felf,
But full of Glory, as thofe Lamps of Heav'n
That fee not, when they fhine.

Em. What is this Heav'n, and Stars, and Night, and Day,
To which you thus compare my Eyes and me?
I underftand you, when you fay you love:
For, when my Father clafps my Hand in his,
That's cold, and I can feel it hard and wrinkl'd;
But when you grafp it, then I figh and pant,
And fomething fmarts, and tickles at my Heart.

Arth. Oh Artlefs Love! where the Soul moves the Tongue,
And only Nature fpeaks what Nature thinks!
Had fhe but Eyes!

Em. Juft now you faid I had:
I fee 'em, I have two.

Arth. But neither fee.

Em. I'm fure they hear you then:
What can your Eyes do more?

Arth. They view your Beauties.

Em. Do not I fee? You have a Face, like mine,
Two Hands, and two round, pretty, rifing Breafts,
That heave like mine.

Arth. But you defcribe a Woman.
Nor is it fight, but touching with your Hands.

Em. Then 'tis my Hand that fees, and that's all one:
For is not feeing, touching with your Eyes?

Arth. No, for I fee at diftance, where I touch not.

Em. If you can fee fo far, and yet not touch,
I fear you fee my Naked Legs and Feet
Quite through my Cloaths; pray do not fee fo well.

Arth. Fear not; fweet Innocence;

                                     D

I view the lovely Features of your Face ;
Your Lips Carnation, your dark fhaded Eye-brows,
Black Eyes, And Snow white Forehead ; all the Colours
That make your Beauty, and produce my Love.

    Em. Nay, then, you do not love on equal terms :
I love you dearly, without all thefe helps :
I cannot fee your Lips Carnation,
Your fhaded Eye-brows, nor your Milk-white Eyes.

    Arth. You ftill miftake.

    Em. Indeed I thought you had a Nofe and Eyes,
And fuch a Face as mine; have not Men Faces ?

    Arth. Oh, none like yours, fo excellently fair.

    Em. Then wou'd I had no Face ; for I wou'd be
Juft fuch a one as you.

    Arth. Alas, 'tis vain to inftruct your Innocence,
You have no Notion of Light or Colours.

    Emmel. Why, is not that a Trumpet ? *(Trumpet found within*

    Arth. Yes.

    Em. I knew it.
And I can tell you how the found on't looks;
It looks as if it had an angry fighting Face.

    Arth. 'Tis now indeed a fharp unpleafant found,
Becaufe it calls me hence, from her I love,
To meet Ten thoufand Foes.

    Em. How does fo many Men ee'r come to meet?
This Devil Trumpet vexes 'em, and then
They feel about, for one anothers Faces ;
And fo they meet, and kill.

    Arth. I'll tell ye all, when we have gain'd the Field ;
One kifs of your fair Hand, the pledge of Conqueft,
And fo a fhort farewel.   { *Kiffes her Hand, and* Exit *with*
                                 { Aurel. Alb. *and Attendants.*

    Em. My Heart, and Vows, go with him to the Fight :
May every Foe, be that, which they call blind,
And none of all their Swords have Eyes to find him.
But lead me nearer to the Trumpet's Face ;
For that brave Sound upholds my fainting Heart ;
And while I hear, methinks I fight my part.
                              (Exit. led by Matilda.

Enter Ofwald and Ofmond.

The Scene reprefents a place of Heathen worfhip; The three Saxon Gods, Woden, Thor, *and* Freya *placed on Pedeftals. An Altar.*

Ofmo. 'Tis time to haften our myfterious Rites;
Becaufe your Army waits you.

Ofwald making three Bows before the three Images.
Ofwa. Thor, Freya, *Woden,* all ye Saxon Powers,
Hear and revenge my Father *Hengift's* death.

Ofmo. Father of Gods and Men, great *Woden,* hear.
Mount thy hot Courfer, drive amidft thy Foes;
Lift high thy thund'ring Arm, let every blow
Dafh out a mif-believing Briton's Brains.

Ofwa. Father of Gods and Men, great *Woden* hear;
Give Conqueft to thy Saxon Race, and me.

Ofmo. Thor, Freya, *Woden,* hear, and fpell your Saxons,
With Sacred Runick Rhimes, from Death in Battle.
Edge their bright Swords, and blunt the Britons Darts.
No more, Great Prince, for fee my trufty Fiend,
Who all the Night has wing'd the dusky Air.

Grimbald, a fierce earthy Spirit arifes.
What news, my *Grimbald?*

Grim. I have plaid my part;
For I have Steel'd the Fools that are to dye;
Six Fools, fo prodigal of Life and Soul,
That, for their Country, they devote their Lives
A Sacrifice to Mother Earth, and *Woden.*

Ofmo. 'Tis well; But are we fure of Victory?
Grim. Why ask'ft thou me?
Infpect their Intrails, draw from thence thy Guefs:
Bloud we muft have, without it we are dumb.

Ofmo. Say, Where's thy fellow-fervant, *Philidel?*
Why comes not he?

Grim. For, he's a puleing Sprite.
Why didft thou chufe a tender airy Form,
Unequal to the mighty work of Mifchief;
His Make is flitting, foft, and yielding Atomes:
He trembles at the yawning gulph of Hell,
Nor dares approach the Flame, left he fhou'd finge
His gaudy filken Wings.

He

He fighs when he fhould plunge a Soul in Sulphur,
As with Compaffion, touch'd of foolifh man.

Ofm. What a half Devil's he?
His Errand was, to draw the Low-land damps,
And Noifom vapours, from the foggy Fens:
Then, breath the baleful ftench, with all his force,
Full on the faces of our Chriftned Foes.

Grim. Accordingly he drein'd thofe Marfhy-grounds ;
And bagg'd 'em in a blue peftiferous Cloud ;
Which when he fhou'd have blown, the frighted Elf
Efpy'd the Red Crofs Banners of their Hoft ;
And faid he durft not add to his damnation.

Ofm. I'le punifh him at leifure ;
Call in the Victims to propitiate Hell.

Grim. That's my kind Mafter, I fhall break faft on 'em.

> *Grimbald goes to the Door, and
> Re-enters with 6 Saxons in
> White, with Swords in their
> hands. They range themfelves
> 3 and 3 in oppofition to each
> other.*

The reft of the Stage is fill'd with Priefts and Singers.

WOden, *firft to thee,*
A Milk white Steed, in Battle won,
We have Sacrific'd.

Chor.　VVe have Sacrific'd.

Verf.　*Let our next Oblation be,*
To Thor, *thy thundring Son,*
Of fuch another.

Chor.　We have Sacrific'd.

Verf.　*A third; (of* Friezeland *breed was he,)*
To Woden's *Wife, and to* Thor's *Mother;*
And now we have atton'd all three
We have Sacrific'd.

Chor.　VVe have Sacrific'd.

The

2 Voc.   *The VVhite Horfe Neigh'd aloud.*
           To VVoden thanks we render.
           To VVoden, we have vow'd.
Chor.   *To VVoden, our Defender.*

                  { The four laſt Lines
                  { in *CHORUS.*

Verſ.   *The Lot is Caſt, and* Tanfan *pleas'd:*
Chor.   *Of Mortal Cares you ſhall be eas'd,*
           Brave Souls to be renown'd in Story.
           Honour prizing,
           Death defpifing,
           Fame acquiring
           By Expiring,
           Dye, and reap the fruit of Glory.
           Brave Souls to be renown'd in Story.

Verſ.   2. *I call ye all,*
           To VVoden's Hall;
           Your Temples round
           VVith Ivy bound,
           In Goblets Crown'd,
           And plenteous Bowls of burniſh'd Gold;
           VVhere you ſhall Laugh,
           And dance and quaff,
           The Juice, that makes the Britons bold.

The ſix Saxons are led off by the Prieſts, in
Order to be Sacrific'd.

Oſſ. Ambitious Fools we are,
And yet Ambition is a Godlike Fault:
Or rather, 'tis no Fault in Souls Born great,
Who dare extend their Glory by their Deeds.
Now *Britany* prepare to change thy State,
And from this Day begin thy Saxon date.

                         [*Exeunt Omnes*

A Battle suppofed to be given behind the Scenes, with Drums, Trumpets, and Military Shouts and Excurfions: After which, the *Britons*, expreffing their Joy for the Victory, fing this Song of Triumph.

COme if you dare, our Trumpets found;
   Come if you dare, the Foes rebound:
We come, we come, we come, we come,
Says the double, double, double Beat of the Thun-
                      (dring Drum:

  Now they charge on amain,
  Now they rally again:
The Gods from above the Mad Labour behold,
And pity Mankind that will perifh for Gold.

The Fainting Saxons quit their Ground,
Their Trumpets Languifh in the Sound;
They fly, they fly, they fly, they fly;
Victoria, Victoria, the Bold Britons cry.

  Now the Victory's won,
  To the Plunder we run:
We return to our Laffes like Fortunate Traders,
Triumphant with Spoils of the Vanquifh'd Invaders.

C   ACT

Enter Philidel.

Phil. ALas, for pity, of this bloody Field!
Piteous it needs muſt be, when I, a Spirit,
Can have ſo ſoft a ſenſe of Humane Woes!
Ah! for ſo many Souls, as but this Morn'
Were cloath'd with Fleſh, and warm'd with Vital Blood,
But naked now, or ſhirted but with Air.

[Merlin, *with Spirits, deſcends to* Philidel,
on a Chariot drawn by Dragons.

Mer. What art thou, Spirit, of what Name and Order?
(For I have view'd thee in my Magick Glaſs,)
Making thy moan, among the Midnight Wolves,
That Bay the ſilent Moon: Speak, I Conjure thee.
'Tis Merlin bids thee, at whoſe awful Wand,
The pale Ghoſt quivers, and the grim Fiend gaſps.

Phil. An Airy Shape, the tender'ſt of my kind,
The laſt ſeduc'd, and leaſt deform'd of Hell;
Half white, and ſhuffl'd in the Crowd, I fell;
Deſirous to repent, and loth to ſin,
Awkward in Miſchief, piteous of Mankind,
My Name is *Philidel,* my Lot in Air,
Where next beneath the Moon, and neareſt Heav'n,
I ſoar; and have a Glimpſe to be receiv'd,
For which the ſwarthy Dæmons envy me.

Mer. Thy Buſineſs here?

Phil. To ſhun the Saxon Wizards dire Commands,
Oſmond, the awful'ſt Name next thine below,
'Cauſe I refus'd to hurl a Noyſom Fog
On Chriſten'd Heads, the Hue and Cry of Hell
Is rais'd againſt me, for a Fugitive Spright.

Mer. *Oſmond* ſhall know, a greater Power protects thee;

But

But follow thou the Whispers of thy Soul,
That draw thee nearer Heav'n.
And, as thy place is nearest to the Sky,
The Rays will reach thee first, and bleach thy Soot.

Phil. In hope of that, I spread my Azure Wings,
And wishing still, for yet I dare not pray,
I bask in Day-light, and behold with Joy
My Scum work outward, and my Rust wear off.

Mer. Why, 'tis my hopeful Devil; now mark me, *Philidel*,
I will employ thee, for thy future Good:
Thou know'st, in spite of Valiant *Oswald's* Arms,
Or *Osmond's* Powerful Spells, the Field is ours. ——

Phil. Oh Master! hasten
Thy Dread Commands; for *Grimbald* is at Hand;
Osmond's fierce Fiend, I snuff his Earthy Scent:
The Conquering *Britons*, he misleads to Rivers,
Or dreadful Downfalls of unheeded Rocks;
Where many fall, that ne'er shall rise again.

Mer. Be that thy care, to stand by falls of Brooks,
And trembling Bogs, that bear a Green-Sword show.
Warn off the bold Pursuers from the Chace:
No more, they come, and we divide the Task.
But left fierce *Grimbald's* pond'rous Bulk oppress
Thy tender flitting Air, I'll leave my Band
Of Spirits with United Strength to Aid thee,
And Force with Force repel.

      Exit Merlin *on his Chariot.*
       Merlin's *Spirits stay with*
       Philidel.

Enter Grimbald *in the Habit of a Shepherd, follow'd by King*
 Arthur, Conon, *Aurelius,* Albanact *and Soldiers,*
  who wander at a distance in the Scenes.

Grim. Here, this way, *Britons,* follow *Oswala's* flight;
This Evening as I whistl'd out my Dog,
To drive my straggling Flock, and pitch'd my Fold,
I saw him dropping Sweat, o'er labour'd, stiff,
Make faintly as he could, to yonder Dell.
Tread in my Steps; long Neighbourhood by Day
      C 2   Has

Has made thefe Fields familiar in the Night.
Arth. I thank thee, Shepherd ;
Expect Reward, lead on, we follow thee.

Phil.   *Hither this way, this way bend,*
fings.   *Truft not that Malicious Fiend :*
          Thofe are falfe deluding Lights,
          Wafted far and near by Sprights.
          Truft 'em not, for they'll deceive ye ;
          And in Bogs and Marfhes leave ye.

Chor. of Phil. Spirits.   *Hither this way, this way bend.*

Chor. of Grimb. Spirits.   *This way, this way bend.*

Phil.   *If you ftep, no Danger thinking,*
fings.   *Down you fall, a Furlong finking :*
          'Tis a Fiend who has annoy'd ye ;
          Name but Heav'n, and he'll avoid ye.

Chor. of Phil. Spirits.   *Hither this way, this way bend.*

Chor. of Grimb. Spirits.   *This way, this way bend.*

Philidels Spirits.   *Truft not that Malicious Fiend.*

Grimbalds Spirits.   *Truft me, I am no Malicious Fiend.*

Philidels Spirits.   *Hither this way,* &c.

    Con. Some wicked Phantom, Foe to Human kind,
Mifguides our Steps.
    Alba. I'll follow him no farther.
    Grimbald fpeaks By Hell fhe fings 'em back, in my defpight.
I had a Voice in Heav'n, ere Sulph'rous Steams
Had damp'd it to a hoarfenefs ; but I'll try.

                                          He

He sings. *Let not a Moon-born Elf mislead ye,*
From your Prey, and from your Glory.
Too far, Alas, he has betray'd ye:
Follow the Flames, that wave before ye:
Sometimes sev'n, and sometimes one;
Hurry, hurry, hurry, hurry on.

2.

See, see, the Footsteps plain appearing,
That way Oswald chose for flying:
Firm is the Turff, and fit for bearing,
Where yonder Pearly Dews are lying.
Far he cannot hence be gone;
Hurry, hurry, hurry, hurry on.

Aur. 'Tis true, he says; the Footsteps yet are fresh
Upon the Sod, no falling Dew-Drops have
Disturb'd the Print.   [*All are going to follow* Grimbald.

Philidel sings. *Hither this way.*

Chor. of Phil. Spirits. *Hither this way, this way bend.*

Chor. of Grimb. Spirits. *This way, this way bend.*

Philidels Spirits. *Trust not that Malicious Fiend.*

Grimb. Spirits. *Trust me, I am no Malicious Fiend.*

Philidels Spirits. *Hither this way,* &c.

They all incline to Philidel.

Grimb.

Grim. speaks. Curse on her Voice, I must my Prey forego;
Thou, *Philidel,* shalt answer this, below.
           [Grimbald *sinks with a Flash.*

Arth. At last the Cheat is plain;
The Cloven-footed Fiend is Vanish'd from us;
Good *Angels* be our Guides, and bring us back.

Phil. singing. *Come follow, follow, follow me.*

Chor. *Come follow,* &c.

    And me. And me. And me. And me.

Vers. 2 Voc. *And Green-Sword all your way shall be.*

Chor. *Come follow,* &c.

Vers. *No* Goblin *or* Elf *shall dare to offend ye.*

Chor. *No, no, no,* &c.
    No Goblin *or* Elf *shall dare to offend ye.*

Vers. 3 Voc. *VVe Brethren of Air,*
   You Hero's will bear,
     To the Kind and the Fair that attend ye.

Chor. *VVe Brethren,* &c.

                Philidel *and the Spirits go off singing, with*
                   King Arthur *and the rest in the middle*
                   of them.

     Enter Emmeline *led by* Matilda. *Pavilion Scene.*

Em. No News of my Dear Love, or of my Father?
Mat. None, Madam, since the gaining of the Battel;
Great *Arthur* is a Royal Conqueror now,
And well deserves your Love.
Em. But now I fear
He'll be too great, to love poor silly me.

                                   If

If he be dead, or never come agen,
I mean to die: But there's a greater doubt,
Since I ne'er faw him here,
How fhall I meet him in another World?

    Mat. I have heard fomething, how two Bodies meet,
But how Souls joyn, I know not.

    Em. I fhou'd find him,
For furely I have feen him in my Sleep,
And then, methought, he put his Mouth to mine,
And eat a thoufand Kiffes on my Lips;
Sure by his Kiffing I cou'd find him out
Among a thoufand Angels in the Sky.

    Mat. But what a kind of Man do you fuppofe him?

    Em. He muft be made of the moft precious things.:
And I believe his Mouth, and Eyes, and Cheeks,
And Nofe, and all his Face, are made of Gold.

    Mat. Heav'n blefs us, Madam, what a Face you make him.
If it be yellow, he muft have the Jaundies,
And that's a bad Difeafe.

    Em. Why then do Lovers give a thing fo bad
As Gold, to Women, whom fo well they love?

    Mat. Becaufe that bad thing, Gold, buys all good things.

    Em. Yet I muft know him better: Of all Colours,
Tell me which is the pureft, and the fofteft.

    Mat. They fay 'tis Black.

    Em. Why then, fince Gold is hard, and yet is precious,
His Face muft all be made of foft, black Gold.

    Mat. But, Madam———

    Em. No more; I have learn'd enough for once.

    Mat. Here are a Crew of Kentifh Lads and Laffes
Wou'd entertain ye, till your Lord's return,
With Songs and Dances, to divert your Cares.

    Em. O bring 'em in,
For tho' I cannot fee the Songs, I love 'em;
And Love, they tell me, is a Dance of Hearts.

Enter

1 Shep- *How blest are Shepherds, how happy their Lasses,*
herd *While Drums & Trumpets are sounding Alarms!*
sings. *Over our Lowly Sheds all the Storm passes;*
    And when we die, 'tis in each others Arms.
    All the Day on our Herds, and Flocks employing;
    All the Night on our Flutes, and in enjoying.
Chor. *All the Day,* &c.

2.

  Bright Nymphs of Britain, with Graces attended,
  Let not your Days without Pleasure expire;
  Honour's but empty, and when Youth is ended,
  All Men will praise you, but none will desire.
  Let not Youth fly away without Contenting;
  Age will come time enough, for your Repenting.
Chor. *Let not Youth,* &c.

Here the Men offer their Flutes to the Women, which they refuse.

2 Shep- *Shepherd, Shepherd, leave Decoying,*
herdess. *Pipes are sweet, a Summers Day;*
    But a little after Toying,
    Women have the Shot to Pay.

2.

  Here are Marriage-Vows for signing,
   Set their Marks that cannot write:
  After that, without Repining,
   Play and Welcom, Day and Night.

Here the Women give the Men Contracts, which they accept.

           Chor.

Chor. } *Come, Shepherds, lead up, a lively Measure;*
of all. } *The Cares of Wedlock, are Cares of Pleasure:*
But whether Marriage bring Joy, or Sorrow,
Make sure of this Day, and hang to Morrow.

The Dance after the Song, and Exeunt
Shepherds and Shepherdesses.

Enter on the other side of the Stage, Ofwald and Guillamar.

Ofw. The Night has wilder'd us; and we are fal'n
Among their foremost Tents.

Guill. Ha! What are thefe!
They feem of more than Vulgar Quality.

Em. What Sounds are thofe? They cannot far be diftant:
Where are we now, *Matilda* ?

Mat. Juft before your Tent:
Fear not, they muft be Friends, and they approach.

Em. My *Arthur*, fpeak, my Love; Are you return'd
To blefs your *Emmeline* ?

Ofwa. to Guilla. I know that Face:
'Tis my Ungrateful Fair, who, fcorning mine,
Accepts my Rivals Love: Heav'n, thou'rt bounteous,
Thou ow'ft me nothing now.

Mat. Fear grows upon me:
Speak what you are; fpeak, or I call for help.

Ofwa. We are your Guards.

Mat. Ah me! We are betray'd; 'tis *Ofwala*'s Voice.

Em. Let 'em not fee our Voices, and then they cannot find us.

Ofw. Paffions in Men Oppress'd, are doubly ftrong.
I take her from King *Arthur*; there's Revenge:
If fhe can love, fhe buoys my finking Fortunes:
Good Reafons both. I'll on. —— Fear nothing, Ladies,
You fhall be fafe. *Ofwald and Guillamar feize Em-*
meline and Matilda.

Em. & Matil. Help, help; a Rape, a Rape!

Ofwa. By Heav'n ye injure me, tho Force is us'd,
Your Honour fhall be facred.

Em. Help, help, Oh *Britons*. help!

Ofwa. Your *Britons* cannot help you:

D This

This Arm, through all their Troops, shall force my way;
Yet neither quit my Honour, nor my Prey.

Exeunt, the Women still crying.

*An Alarm within: Some Soldiers running over the
Stage: Follow, follow, follow.*

Enter Albanact Captain of the Guards, with Soldiers.

Alb. Which way went th' Alarm?
1. *Sol.* Here, towards the Castle,
Alb. Pox o' this Victory; the whole Camp's debauch'd:
All Drunk or Whoring: This way, follow, follow. *Exeunt.*
The Alarm renews: Clashing of Swords within for a while.

Re-enter Albanact, Officer and Soldiers.

Officer. How fits the Conquest on great *Arthur's* Brow?
Alba. As when the Lover, with the King is mixt,
He puts the gain of *Britain* in a Scale,
Which weighing with the loss of *Emmeline*,
He thinks he's scarce a Saver.   *Trumpet within.*
Officer. Hark! a Trumpet!
It sounds a Parley.
Alba. 'Tis from *Oswald* then,
An Eccho to King *Arthur's* Friendly Summons,
Sent since he heard the Rape of *Emmeline*,
To ask an Interview.   *Trumpet answering on the other side.*
Officer. But hark! already
Our Trumpet makes reply; and see both present.

*Enter Arthur on one side attended, Oswald on the other
with Attendants, and Guillamar. They
meet and salute.*

Arthur. Brave *Oswald!* We have met on Friendlier Terms,
Companions of a War, with Common Interest
Against the Bordering *Picts:* But Times are chang'd.
Oswa. And I am sorry that those Times are chang'd:
For else we now might meet, on Terms as Friendly.

Aith. If

Arth. If fo we meet not now, the fault's your own;
For you have wrong'd me much.

Ofwa. Oh you wou'd tell me,
I call'd more *Saxons* in, t' enlarge my Bounds:
If thofe be Wrongs, the War has well redrefs'd ye.

Arth. Miftake me not, I count not War a Wrong:
War is the Trade of Kings, that fight for Empire;
And better be a Lyon, than a Sheep.

Ofwa. In what, then, have I wrong'd ye?

Arth. In my Love.

Ofwa. Even Love's an Empire too; The Noble Soul,
Like Kings, is Covetous of fingle Sway.

Arth. I blame ye not, for loving *Emmeline*:
But fince the Soul is free, and Love is choice,
You fhou'd have made a Conqueft of her Mind,
And not have forc'd her Perfon by a Rape.

Ofwa. Whether by Force, or Stratagem, we gain;
Still Gaining is our End, in War or Love.
Her Mind's the Jewel, in her Body lock'd;
If I would gain the Gem, and want the Key,
It follows I muft feize the Cabinet:
But to fecure your fear, her Honour is untouch'd.

Arth. Was Honour ever fafe in Brutal Hands?
So fafe are Lambs within the Lyons Paw;
Ungrip'd and plaid with, till fierce Hunger calls,
Then Nature fhews it felf; the clofe-hid Nails
Are ftretch'd, and open'd, to the panting Prey.
But if indeed, you are fo Cold a Lover ——

Ofwa. Not Cold, but Honourable.

Arth. Then Reftore her.
That done, I fhall believe you Honourable.

Ofwa. Think'ft thou I will forego a Victor's Right?

Arth. Say rather, of an Impious Ravifher.
That Caftle, were it wall'd with *Adamant*,
Can hide thy Head, but till to Morrow's Dawn.

Ofwa. And ere to Morrow, I may be a God,
If *Emmeline* be kind: But kind or cruel,
I tell thee, *Arthur*, but to fee this Day,
That Heavenly Face, tho' not to have her mine,
I would give up a hundred Years of Life,

{And

And bid Fate cut to Morrow.

Arth. It soon will come, and thou repent too late,
Which to prevent, I'll bribe thee to be honest:
Thy Noble Head, accustom'd to a Crown,
Shall wear it still : Nor shall thy Hand forget
The Sceptre's use : From *Medway*'s pleasing Stream,
To *Severn*'s Roar, be thine.
In short, Restore my Love, and share my Kingdom.

Osw. Not, tho' you spread my Sway from *Thames* to *Tyber* ;
Such Gifts might bribe a King, but not a Lover.

Arth. Then prithee give me back my Kingly Word,
Pass'd for thy safe return ; and let this Hour,
In single Combat, Hand to Hand, decide
The Fate of Empire, and of *Emmelin*.

Osw. Not, that I fear, do I decline this Combat ;
And not decline it neither, but defer :
When *Emmeline* has been my Prize as long
As she was thine, I dare thee to the Duel.

Arth. I nam'd your utmost Term of Life ; To Morrow.
Osw. You are not Fate.
Arth. But Fate is in this Arm.
You might have made a Merit of your Theft.
Osw. Ha! Theft! Your Guards can tell, I stole her not.
Arth. Had I been present———
Osw. Had you been present, she had been mine more Nobly.
Arth. There lies your way.
Osw. My way lies where I please.
Expect (for *Oswald*'s Magick cannot fail)
A long To Morrow, ere your Arms prevail :
Or if I fall, make Room ye blest above,
For one who was undone, and dy'd for Love.

Exit Oswald and his Party.

Arth. There may be one black Minute ere To Morrow :
For who can tell, what Pow'r, and Lust, and Charms,
May do this Night ? To Arms, with speed, to Arms.

Exit.

ACT III.

Enter Arthur, Conon *and* Aurelius.

Con. FUrle up our Colours, and Unbrace our Drums;
D.llodge betimes ; and quit this fatal Coaft.
Arth. Have we forgot to Conquer ?
Aurel. Caft off Hope :
Th' Imbattl'd Legions of Fire, Air, and Earth,
Are banded for our Foes.
For .c'n ; to difcover, with the Dawn,
Yon Southern Hill, which promis'd to the Sight
A Rife more eafie to attack the Fort,
Scarce had we ftept on the Forbidden Ground,
When the Woods fhook, the Trees ftood briftling up ;
A Living Trembling Nodded through the Leaves.
   Arth. Poplars, and Afpen-Boughs, a Pannick Fright.
   Conon. We thought fo too, and doubled ftil! our pace.
But ftrait a rumbling Sound, like bellowing Winds,
Rofe and grew loud ; Confus'd with Howls of Wolves,
And Grunts of Bears; and dreadful Hifs of Snakes :
Shreiks more than Humane ; Globes of Hail pour'd down
An Armed Winter, and Inverted Day.
   Arth. Dreadful indeed !
   Aur. Count then our Labour's loft :
For other way lies none, to mount the Cliff,
Unlefs we borrow Wings, and fail thro' Air.
   Arth. Now I perceive a Danger worthy me.
'Tis *Ofmond's* Work, a Band of Hell-hir'd Slaves :
Be mine the Hazard, mine fhall be the Fame.

Arthur *is going out, but is met by* Merlin,
who takes him by the Hand, and brings
him back.

Enter

Enter Merlin.

{dangerous ;

Merl. Hold, Sir, and wait Heav'ns time ; th' *Attempts* too
There's not a Tree in that Inchanted Grove,
But numbred out, and given by tale to Fiends ;
And under every Leaf a Spirit couch'd.
But by what Method to diffolve thefe Charms,
Is yet unknown to me.

Arth. Hadft thou been here, (for what can thwart thy Skill?)
Nor *Emmeline* had been the boaft of *Ofwald* ;
Nor I fore-warn'd, been wanting to her Guard.

Con. Her darkn'd Eyes had feen the Light of *Heav'n* ;
That was thy promife too, and this the time.

Mer. Nor has my *Aid* been abfent, tho' unfeen,
With Friendly Guides in your benighted Maze :
Nor *Emmeline* fhall longer want the Sun.

Arth. Is there an end of Woes?

Merl. There is, and fudden.
I have employ'd a fubtil *Airy* Spright,
T' explore the paffage, and prepare my way.
My felf, mean time, will view the Magick Wood,
To learn whereon depends its Force.

Con. But *Emmeline* ——

Mer. Fear not : This Vial fhall reftore her fight.

Arth. Oh might I hope (and what's impoffible
To *Merlin*'s Art) to be my felf the Bearer,
That with the Light of *Heav'n* fhe may difcern
Her Lover firft.

Mer. 'Tis wondrous hazardous ;
Yet I forefee th' Event, 'tis fortunate.
I'll bear ye fafe, and bring ye back unharm'd :
Then lofe not precious Time, but follow me.

Exeunt Omnes, Merlin *leading* Arthur.

Enter Philidel.   *Scene, a Deep Wood.*

Phi. I left all fafe behind ;
For in the hindmoft quarter of the Wood,
My former Lord, Grim *Ofmond,* walks the Round :

Calls

Calls o'er the Names, and Schools the tardy Sprights.
His Abfence gives me more fecurity.
At every Walk I pafs'd, I drew a Spell,
So that if any Fiend, abhorring Heav'n,
There fets his Foot, it roots him to the Ground.
Now cou'd I but difcover *Emmeline*,
My Task were fairly done.   [*Walking about, and Prying
betwixt the Trees.*]

    Enter Grimbald *rufhing out : He feizes* Philidel, *and
binds him in a Chain.*

    Grimb. O Rebel, have I caught thee !
    Phil. Ah me ! What hard mifhap !
    Grimb. What juft Revenge !
Thou mifcreant Elf, thou Renegado Scout,
So clean, fo furbifh'd, fo renew'd in White,
The Livery of our Foes ; I fee thee through :
What mak'ft thou here ? Thou trim Apoftate, fpeak,
Thou fhak'ft for Fear, I feel thy falfe Heart Pant.
    Phil. Ah mighty *Grimbald,*
Who would not Fear, when feiz'd in thy ftrong Grip ;
But here me, Oh Renown'd, Oh worthy Fiend,
The Favourite of our Cheif.
    Grimb. Away with fullfome Flattery,
The Food of Fools ; thou know'ft where laft we met,
When but for thee, the Chriftians had been fwallow'd
In quaking Bogs, and Living fent to Hell.
    Phil. Aye, then I was feduc'd by *Merlin*'s Art,
And half perfuaded by his foothing Tales,
To hope for Heav'n ; as if Eternal Doom
Cou'd be Revers'd, and undecreed for me :
But I am now fet Right.
    Grimb. Oh ftill thou think'ft to fly a Fool to Mark.
    Phil. I fled from *Merlin*, free as Air that bore me,
T'unfold to *Ofmond* all his deep Defigns.
    Grimb. I believe nothing, Oh thou fond Impoftor,
When wert thou laft in Hell ? Is not thy Name
Forgot, and Blotted from th' Infernal Roll ;
But fince thou fay'ft, thy Errand was to *Ofmond,*

Tis.

To *Ofmond* fha'lt thou go ; March, know thy Driver.

Phil. Kneeling. Oh fpare me *Grimbald,* and I'll be thy Slave;
Tempt Hermits for thee, in their Holy Cells,
And Virgins in their Dreams.

Grimb. Canft thou, a Devil, hope to cheat a Devil?
A Spy ; why that's a Name abhorr'd in Hell ;
Hafte forward, forward, or I'll Goad thee on,
With Iron Spurrs.

Phil. But ufe me kindly then :
Pull not fo hard, to hurt my Airy Limbs;
I'll follow thee unforc'd ; look, there's thy way.

Grimb. Ay, there's the way indeed ; but for more furety
I'll keep an Eye behind: Not one Word more,
But follow decently.   *Grimbald goes out, dragging* Philidel.

Phil. afide. So, catch him Spell.

Grimb. within. Oh help me, help me, *Philidel.*

Phil. Why, What's the matter?

Grimb. Oh, I am enfnar'd ;
Heav'ns Birdlime wraps me round, and glues my Wings.
Lofe me, and I will free thee ;
Do, and I'll be thy Slave.

Phil. What, to a Spy, a Name abhort'd in Hell ?

Grimb. Do not infult, Oh, Oh, I grow to Ground ;
The Fiery Net draws clofer on my Limbs.

Phil. Thou fhalt not have the Eafe to Curfe in Torments :
Be Dumb for one half Hour; fo long my Charm
Can keep thee Silent, and there lie
Till *Ofmond* breaks thy Chain.
                    Philidel *unbinds his own Fetters.*

Enter to him Merlin, *with a Vial in his Hand ; and* Arthur.

Mer. Well haft thou wrought thy Safety with thy Wit,
My *Philidel* ; go Meritorious on.
Me, other Work requires, to view the Wood,
And learn to make the dire Inchantments void.
Mean time attend King *Arthur* in my Room ;
Shew him his Love, and with thefe Soveraign Drops,
Reftore her Sight.
                    Exit Merlin *giving a Viol to* Philidel.
                                        Phil.

Phil. *We must work, we must haste ;*
Noon-Tyde Hour, is almost past :
Sprights, that glimmer in the Sun,
Into Shades already run.
Ofmond *will be here, anon.*

Enter Emmeline *and* Matilda, *at the far end of the Wood.*

Arth. O yonder, yonder fhe's already found :
My Soul directs my fight, and flies before it.
Now, Gentle Spirit, ufe thy utmoft Art ;
Unfeal her Eyes ; and this way lead her Steps.
                    Arthur *withdraws behind the Scene.*
            Emmeline *and* Matilda *come forward to the Front.*

Philidel *approaches* Emmeline, *fprinkling fome of the*
Water over her Eyes, out of the Vial.

Phil.   *Thus, thus I infufe*
            Thefe Soveraign Dews.
    Fly back, ye Films, that Cloud her fight,
    And you, ye Chryftal Humours bright,
    Your Noxious Vapours purg'd away,
    Recover, and admit the Day.
    Now caft your Eyes abroad, and fee
        All but me.

Em. Ha ! What was that ? Who fpoke ?
Mat. I heard the Voice ; 'tis one of *Ofmond's* Fiends.
Em. Some bleffed Angel fure ; I feel my Eyes
Unfeal'd, they walk abroad, and a new World
Comes rufhing on, and ftands all gay before me.
Mat. Oh Heavens ! Oh Joy of Joys ! fhe has her fight !
Em. I am new-born ; I fhall run mad for Pleafure.   *Staring*
Are Women fuch as thou ? Such Glorious Creatures ?   *(on* Mat.
                                        Arth.
                        E

Arth. aside. Oh how I envy her, to be firſt ſeen !

Em. Stand farther ; let me take my fill of ſight.   *Looking*
What's that above, that weakens my new Eyes,   *(up.*
Makes me not ſee, by ſeeing ?

Mat. 'Tis the Sun.

Em. The Sun, 'tis ſure a God, if that be Heav'n :
Oh, if thou art a Creature, beſt and faireſt,
How well art thou, from Mortals ſo remote,
To ſhine, and not to burn, by near approach !
How haſt thou light'ned even my very Soul,
And let in Knowledge by another ſenſe !
I gaze about, new-born, to Day and thee ;
A Stranger yet, an Infant of the World !
Art thou not pleas'd, *Matilda* ? Why, like me,
Doſt thou not look and wonder ?

Mat. For theſe Sights
Are to my Eyes familiar.

Em. That's my Joy,
Not to have ſeen before : For Nature now,
Comes all at once, confounding my Delight.
But ah ! what Thing am I ? Fain wou'd I know ;
Or am I blind, or do I ſee but half ?
With all my Care, and looking round about,
I cannot view my Face.

Mat None ſee themſelves
But by Reflection ; in this Glaſs you may.   *Gives her a Glaſs.*

Emm.taking ⎫What's this ?
the Glaſs, and ⎬It holds a Face within it : Oh ſweet Face ;
looking.   ⎭It draws the Mouth, and Smiles, and looks upon
And talks ; but yet I cannot hear it Speak :.   *(me ;*
The pretty thing is Dumb.

Mat. The pretty thing
You ſee within the Glaſs, is you.

Emm. What, Am I two ? Is this another me ?
Indeed it wears my Cloaths, has Hands like mine ;
And Mocks what e'er I do ; but that I'm ſure
I am a Maid, I'd ſwear it were my Child.   Matilda *looks.*
Look my *Matilda* ; We both are in the Glaſs,
Oh, now I know it plain ; they are our Names
That peep upon us there.

Mat. Our Shadows, *Madam.*   *Emm.*

Emm. Mine is a prettier Shaddow far, then thine.
I Love it ; let me Kifs my to'ther Self.   *Kiffing the Glafs,*
Alas, I've kifs'd it Dead; the fine Thing's gone ; *(and hugging it.*
Indeed it Kifs'd fo Cold, as if 'twere Dying.

   Arthur *comes forward foftly ; fhewing himfelf behind her.*
'Tis here again.
Oh no, this Face is neither mine nor thine ;
I think the Glafs has Born another Child.   *She turns and*
Ha ! What art thou with a new kind of Face,   *(fees* Arthur.
And other Cloaths, a Noble Creature too ;
But taller, bigger, fiercer in thy Look ;
Of a Comptrolling Eye, Majeftick make ?

   Mat. Do you not know him, Madam ?

   Emm. Is't a Man ?

   Arth. Yes, And the moft unhappy of my kind,
If you have chang'd your Love.

   Emm. My deareft Lord !
Was my Soul Blind ; and cou'd not that look out,
To know you, e're you Spoke ? Oh Counterpart
Of our foft Sex ; Well are ye made our Lords,
So bold, fo great, fo God-like are ye form'd.
How can ye Love fuch filly Things as Women ?

   Arth. Beauty like yours Commands ; and Man was made
But a more boifterous ; and a ftronger Slave,
To you, the beft Delights of human Kind.

   Emm. But are ye mine ? Is there an end of War ?
Are all thofe Trumpets Dead themfelves, at laft,
That us'd to kill Men with their Thundring Sounds ?

   Arth. The Sum of War is undecided yet ;
And many a breathing Body muft be Cold,
Ere you are free.

   Emm. How came ye hither then ?

   Arth. By *Merlin*'s Art, to fnatch a fhort liv'd Blifs ;
To feed my Famifh'd Love upon your Eyes,
One Moment, and depart.

   Emm. O Moment, worth——
Whole Ages paft, and all that are to come *!*
Let Love-fick *Ofwald*, now, unpitied mourn ;
Let *Ofmond* mutter Charms to Sprights in vain,
To make me Love him ; all fhall not change my Soul.

Arth. Ha! Does the Inchanter practice Hell upon you?
Is he my Rival too?

Emm. Yes, but I hate him;
For when he spoke, through my shut Eyes I saw him;
His Voice look'd ugly, and breath'd Brimstone on me:
And then I first was glad that I was Blind,
Not to behold Damnation.

Phil. This time is left me to Congratulate
Your new-born Eyes; and tell you what you gain
By sight restor'd, and viewing him you love.
Appear, you Airy Forms.   *Airy Spirits appear in the*
                            (Shapes of Men and Women.

Man sings. *Oh Sight, the Mother of Desires,*
    What Charming Objects dost thou yield!
      'Tis sweet, when tedious Night expires,
    To see the Rosie Morning guild
      The Mountain-Tops, and paint the Field!
    But, when Clorinda *comes in sight,*
    She makes the Summers Day more bright;
    And when she goes away, 'tis Night.

Chor. *When Fair* Clorinda *comes in sight,* &c.

Wom. sings. *'Tis sweet the Blushing Morn to view;*
    And Plains adorn'd with Pearly Dew:
    But such cheap Delights to see,
    Heaven and Nature,
    Give each Creature;
    They have Eyes, as well as we.
    This is the Joy, all Joys above,
      To see, to see;
      That only she,
    That only she we love!

Chor. *This is the Joy, all Joys above,* &c.

Man

Man sings. *And, if we may discover,*
    What Charms both Nymph and Lover,
      'Tis, when the Fair at Mercy lies,
    With Kind and Amorous Anguish,
    To Sigh, to Look, to Languish,
      On each others Eyes !

Chor. of all
Men & Wom. } *And if we may discover,* &c.

Phil. Break off your Musick ; for our Foes are near.

                               Spirits vanish.

                Enter Merlin.

   Merl. My Soveraign, we have hazarded too far ;
But Love excuses you, and prescience me.
Make haste ; for *Osmond* is even now alarm'd,
And greedy of Revenge, is hasting home.
   Arth. Oh take my Love with us, or leave me here.
   Merl. I cannot, for she's held by Charms too strong:
Which, with th' Inchanted Grove must be destroy'd ;
Till when, my Art is vain: But fear not, *Emmeline* ;
Th' Enchanter has no Pow'r on Innocence.
   *Em.*to*Arth.*Farewel,Since we must part:When you are gone,
I'll look into my Glass, just where you look'd ;
To find your Face again ;
If 'tis not there, I'll think on you so long,
My Heart shall make your Picture for my Eyes.
   Arth. Where-e'er I go, my Soul shall stay with thee :
'Tis but my Shadow that I take away ;
True Love is never happy but by halves ;
An *April* Sun-Shine, that by fits appears,
It smiles by Moments, but it mourns by Years.

              Exeunt Arthur *and* Merlin *at one Door.*

                                  Enter

Enter Ofmond *at the other Door, who gazes on* Emmeline, *and fhe on him.*

Emm. Matilda fave me, from this ugly Thing,
This Foe to fight, Speak, doft thou know him:
  Matil. Too well ; 'tis Ofwala's Friend, the great Magician.
  Emm. It cannot be a Man, he's fo unlike the Man I Love.
  Ofm. afiae. Death to my Eyes, fhe fees!
  Emm. I wifh I cou'd not ; but I'll clofe my Sight,
And fhut out all I can —— It wo'not be ;
Winking, I fee thee ftill, thy odious Image
Stares full into my Soul ; and there infects the Room
My Arthur fhou'd poffefs.
  Ofm. afide. I find too late,
That Merlin and her Lover have been here.
If I was fir'd before, when fhe was Blind,
Her Eyes dart Lightning now, fhe muft be mine.
  Emm. I prithee Dreadful Thing, tell me thy Bufinefs here
And if thou canft, Reform that odious Face ;
Look not fo Grim upon me.
  Ofm. My Name is Ofmond, and my Bufinefs Love.
  Emm. Thou haft a griezly look ; forbidding what thou askt,
If I durft tell thee fo.
  Ofm. My Pent-Houfe Eye-Brows, and my Shaggy Beard
Ofiend your Sight, but thefe are Manly Signs;
Faint White and Red, abufe your Expectations ;
Be Woman ; know your Sex, and Love full Pleafures.
  Emm. Love from a Monfter, Fiend !
  Ofm. Come you muft Love, or you muft fuffer Love ;
No Coinefs, None, for I am Mafter here.
  Emm. And when did Ofwald give away his Power,
That thou prefum'ft to Rule ? Be fure I'll tell him :
For as I am his Prifoner, he is mine.
  Ofm. Why then thou art a Captive to a Captive,
O'er labour'd with the Fight, oppreft with Thirft ;
That Ofwald whom you mention'd call'd for Drink :
I mix'd a Sleepy Potion in his Bowl ;
Which he and his Fool Friend, quaff'd greedily ,
The happy Dofe wrought the defir'd effect ;
Then to a Dungeons depth, I fent both Bound :

                        Where

Where ftow'd with Snakes and Adders now they lodge ;
Two Planks their Beds ; Slippery with Oofe and Slime :
The Ratts brufh o'er their Faces with their Tails ;
And croaking Paddocks crawl upon their Limbs.
Since when the Garifon depends on me ;
Now know you are my Slave.

Matil. He ftrikes a Horrour through my Blood.

Emm. I Freeze, as if his impious Art had fix'd
My Feet to Earth.

Ofm. But Love fhall thaw ye.
I'll fhow his force in Countries cak'd with Ice,
Where the pale Pole-Star in the North of Heav'n
Sits high, and on the frory Winter broods ;
Yet there Love Reigns : For proof, this Magick Wand
Shall change the Mildnefs of fweet *Britains* Clime
To *Tzeland*, and the fartheft *Thule's* Froft ;
Where the proud God, difdaining Winters Bounds,
O'er-leaps the Fences of Eternal Snow,
And with his Warmth, fupplies the diftant Sun.

> Ofmond *ftrikes the Ground with his Wand : The Scene*
> *changes to a Profpect of Winter in Frozen Countries.*

Cupid *Defcends.*

Cup. fings. *What ho, thou* Genius *of the Clime, what ho !*
Ly'ft thou afleep beneath thofe Hills of Snow ?
Stretch out thy Lazy-Limbs ; Awake, awake,
And Winter from thy Furry Mantle fhake.

Geniüs *Arifes.*

Genius. *VVhat Power art thou, who from below,*
Haft made me Rife, unwillingly, and flow,
From Beds of Everlafting Snow !
Seeft thou not how ftiff, and wondrous old,
Far unfit to bear the bitter Cold,

I can scarcely move, or draw my Breath ;
Let me, let me, Freeze again to Death.

Cupid. Thou Doting Fool, forbear, forbear ;
VVhat, Dost thou Dream of Freezing here ?
At Loves appearing, all the Skie clearing,
    The Stormy VVinds their Fury spare :
VVinter subduing, and Spring renewing,
    My Beams create a more Glorious Year.
Thou Doting Fool, forbear, forbear ;
VVhat, Dost thou Dream of Freezing here ?

Genius. Great Love, I know thee now ;
Eldest of the Gods art Thou :
Heav'n and Earth, by Thee were made.
    Humane Nature,
    Is Thy Creature,
Every where Thou art obey'd.

Cupid. No part of my Dominion shall be waste,
    To spread my Sway, and sing my Praise,
    Ev'n here I will a People raise,
Of kind embracing Lovers, and embrac'd.

Cupid waves his Wand, upon which the Scene opens, and
discovers a Prospect of Ice and Snow to the end of the
Stage.

Singers and Dancers, Men and Women, appears.

Man. See, see, we assemble,
    Thy Revels to hold :
    Though quiv'ring with Cold,
    We Chatter and Tremble.   Cupid.

Cupid. *'Tis I, 'tis I, 'tis I, that have warm'd ye ;*
In spight of Cold Weather,
I've brought ye together :
'Tis I, 'tis I, 'tis I, that have arm'd ye.

Chor. *'Tis Love,'tis Love,'tis Love that has warm'd us;*
In spight of Cold Weather,
He brought us together :
'Tis Love, 'tis Love, 'tis Love that has arm'd us.

Cupid. *Sound a Parley, ye Fair, and surrender ;*
Set your selves, and your Lovers at ease ;
He's a Grateful Offender
Who Pleasure dare seize :
But the Whining Pretender
Is sure to displease.

2.

Since the Fruit of Desire is possessing,
'Tis Unmanly to Sigh and Complain ;
When we Kneel for Redressing,
We move your Disdain :
Love was made for a Blessing,
And not for a Pain.

A Dance ; after which the Singers and Dancers depart.

Emm. I cou'd be pleas'd with any one but thee,
Who entertain'd my sight with such Gay Shows,
As Men and Women moving here and there ;
That Coursing one another in their Steps,
Have made their Feet a Tune.

Ofmo. What, Coying it again !
No more ; but make me happy to my Guft,
That is, without your ftruggling.

Emm. From my fight,
Thou all thy Devils in one, thou dar'ft not force me.

Ofmo. You teach me well, I find you wou'd be Ravifh'd ;
I'll give you that excufe your Sex defires.

He begins to lay hold on her, and they ftruggle.

Grimb. within. O help me, Mafter, help me !

Ofmo. Who's that, my *Grimbald !* Come and help thou me :
For 'tis thy Work t'affift a Ravifher.

Grimb. within. I cannot ftir ; I am Spell-caught by *Phildel*,
And purs'd within a Net: With a huge heavy weight of Holy
Laid on my Head, that keeps me down from rifing.   (Words,

Ofmo. I'll read 'em backwards, and releafe thy Bonds :
Mean time go in : ——   *To Emmeline.*
Prepare your felf, and eafe my Drudgery :
But if you will not fairly be enjoy'd,
A little honeft Force, is well employ'd.   *Exit Ofmond.*

Emm. Heav'n be my Guard, I have no other Friend !
Heav'n ever prefent to thy Suppliants Aid,
Protect and pity Innocence betray'd.
                        Exeunt Emmeline and Matilda.

ACT

ACT IV. SCENE I.

Enter Ofmond Solus.

Now I am fettled in my Force-full Sway;
  Why then, I'll be Luxurious in my Love;
Take my full Guft, and fetting Forms afide,
I'll bid the Slave, that fires my Blood, lie down.

Seems to be going off.

Enter Grimbald, *who meets him.*

Grim. Not fo faft, Mafter, Danger threatens thee:
There's a black Cloud, defcending from above,
Full of Heavens Venom, burfting o'er thy Head.
  Ofmo. Malicious Fiend, thou ly'ft: For I am fenc'd
By Millions of thy Fellows, in my Grove:
I bad thee, when I freed thee from the Charm,
Run fcouting through the Wood, from Tree to Tree,
And look if all my Devils were on Duty:
Hadft thou perform'd thy Charge, thou tardy Spright,
Thou wouldft have known no Danger threatn'd me.
  Grim. When did a Devil fail in Diligence?
Poor Mortal, thou thy felf art overfeen;
I have been there, and thence I bring this News.
Thy Fatal Foe, great *Arthur*, is at hand;
Merlin has ta'en his time while thou wert abfent,
T' obferve thy Charaters, their Force, and Nature,
And Counterwork thy Spells.
  Ofmo. The Devil take *Merlin*;
I'll caft 'em all anew, and inftantly,
All of another Mould; be thou at hand.
Their Compofition was, before, of Horror;
Now they fhall be of Blandifhment, and Love;

Seducing

Seducing Hopes, foft Pity, tender Moans:
Art fhall meet *Art* ; and, when they think to win,
The Fools fhall find their Labour to begin.

Exeunt Ofm- *and* Grimb.

Enter Arthur, and Merlin *at another Door.*

Scene of the Wood continues.

Merl. Thus far it is permitted me to go ;
But all beyond this Spot, is fenc'd with Charms ;
I may no more ; but only with advice.

Arth. My Sword fhall do the reft.

Merl. Remember well, that all is but Illufion ;
Go on ; good Stars attend thee.

Arth. Doubt me not.

Merl. Yet in prevention
Of what may come, I'll leave my *Philidel*
To watch thy Steps, and with him leave my Wand ;
The touch of which, no Earthy Fiend can bear,
In whate'er Shape transform'd, but muft lay down
His borrow'd Figure, and confefs the Devil.
Once more Farewel, and profper.   *Exit Merlin.*

Arth. walking. No Danger yet, I fee no Walls of Fire,
No City of the Fiends, with Forms obfcene,
To grin from far, on Flaming Battlements.
This is indeed the Grove I fhou'd deftroy ;
But where's the Horrour ? Sure the Prophet err'd.
Hark ! Mufick, and the warbling Notes of Birds ;

Soft Mufick.

Hell entertains me, like fome welcom Gueft.
More Wonders yet ; yet all delightful too,
A Silver Current to forbid my paffage,
And yet to invite me, ftands a Golden Bridge :
Perhaps a Trap, for my Unwary Feet
To fink, and whelm me underneath the Waves ;
With Fire or Water, let him wage his VVar,
Or all the Elements at once ; I'll on.

As he is going to the Bridge, two Syrens arife from the
Water ; They fhew themfelves to the Wafte, & fing.

1. Svren.

1 Syren. *O pass not on, but stay,*
And waste the Joyous Day
VVith us in gentle Play:
Unbend to Love, unbend thee:
O lay thy Sword aside,
And other Arms provide;
For other Wars attend thee,
And sweeter to be try'd.

Chor. *For other Wars, &c.*

Both sing. *Two Daughters of this Aged Stream are we;*
And both our Sea-green Locks have comb'd for
Come Bathe with us an Hour or two, (*thee;*
Come Naked in, for we are so;
What Danger from a Naked Foe?
Come Bathe with us, come Bathe, and share,
VVhat Pleasures in the Floods appear;
We'll beat the Waters till they bound,
And Circle, round, around, around,
And Circle round, around.

Arth. A Lazie Pleasure trickles through my Veins;
Here cou'd I stay, and well be Couzen'd here.
But Honour calls; Is Honour in such haste?
Can he not Bait at such a pleasing Inn?
No; for the more I look, the more I long;
Farewel, ye Fair Illusions, I must leave ye,
While I have Power to say, that I must leave ye.
Farewel, with half my Soul I stagger off;
How dear this flying Victory has cost,
When, if I stay to struggle, I am lost.

As he is going forward, Nymphs *and* Sylvans *come out*
from behind the Trees. Base and two Trebles sing
the following Song to a Minuet.

Dance

Dance with the Song, all with Branches in their Hands.

Song.   *How happy the Lover,*
     How easie his Chain,
     How pleasing his Pain?
   How sweet to discover!
   He sighs not in vain.
   For Love every Creature
   Is form'd by his Nature;
   No Joys are above
   The Pleasures of Love.

The Dance continues with the same Measure play'd alone.

2.

   In vain are our Graces,
     In vain are your Eyes,
     If Love you despise;
   When Age furrows Faces,
     'Tis time to be wise.
   Then use the short Blessing,
   That Flies in Possessing:
   No Joys are above
   The Pleasures of Love.

Arth. And what are these Fantastick Fairy Joys,
To Love like mine? False Joys, false Welcomes all.
Begone, ye *Sylvan* Trippers of the Green;
Fly after Night, and overtake the Moon.   *Here the Dancers,*
                      (Singers and Syrens vanish.
This goodly Tree seems Queen of all the Grove.
The Ringlets round her Trunk declare her guilty
Of many Midnight-Sabbaths Revell'd here.
Her will I first attempt.   *Arthur strikes at the Tree, and cuts*
     it; Blood spouts out of it, a Groan follows, then a Shreik.

Good Heav'ns, what Monstrous Prodigies are these!

                                        Blood

Blood follows from my blow ; the wounded Rind
Spouts on my Sword, and Sanguine dyes the Plain.
   He strikes again : A Voice of Emmeline *from behind.*
 Em. from behind. Forbear, if thou haft Pity, ah, forbear !
Thefe Groans proceed not from a Scncelefs Plant,
No Spouts of Blood run welling from a Tree.
 Arth. Speak what thou art ; I charge thee fpeak thy Being ;
Thou that haft made my cúrdl'd Blood run back,
My Heart heave up ; my Hair to rife in Briftles,
And fcarcely left a Voice to ask thy Name.
    Emmeline *breaks out of the Tree*
     fhewing her Arm Bloody.
 Emm. Whom thou haft hurt, Unkind and Cruel fee ;
Look on this Blood, 'tis fatal, ftill, to me
To bear thy Wounds, my Heart has felt 'em firft.
 Arth. 'Tis fhe ; Amazement roots me to the Groun !!
 Emm. By cruel Charms, dragg'd from my pcaceful Bower,
Fierce *Ofmond* clofs'd me in this bleeding Bark ;
And bid me ftand expos'd to the bleak Winds,
And Winter Storms ; and Heav'ns Inclemency,
Bound to the Fate of this Hell-haunted Grove ;
So that whatever Sword, or founding Axe,
Shall violate this Plant, muft pierce my Flefh,
And when that falls, I dye. ———
 Arth. If this be true,
O never, never, to be ended Cha**r**m,
At leaft by me ; yet all may be Illufion.
Break up, ye thickning Foggs, and filmy Mifts,
All that be-lye my Sight, and cheat my Senfe.
For Reafon ftill pronounces, 'tis not fhe,
And thus refolv'd--- *Lifts up his Sword, as going to ftrike.*
 Emm. Do, ftrike Barbarian, ftrike ;
And ftrew my mangl'd Limbs, with every ftroke
Wound me, and double Kill me, with Unkindnefs,
That by thy Hand I fell.
 Arth. What fhall I do, ye Powers?
 Emm. Lay down thy Vengeful Sword ; 'tis fatal here :
What need of Arms, where no Defence is made?
A Love-Sick Virgin, panting with Defire,
No Confcious Eye t'intrude on our Delights:
         Fer

For this thou haſt the *Syren's* Songs deſpis'd ;
For this, thy Faithful Paſſion I Reward ;
Haſte then, to take me longing to thy Arms.
  Arth. O Love ! O *Merlin* ! Whom ſhould I believe ?
  Emm. Believe thy Self, thy Youth, thy Love, and me ;
They only, they, who pleaſe themſelves are Wiſe :
Diſarm thy Hand, that mine may meet it bare.
  Arth. By thy leave, Reaſon, here I throw thee off,
Thou load of Life: If thou wert made for Souls,
Then Souls ſhou'd have been made without their Bodies.
If, falling for the firſt Created Fair,
Was *Adam's* Fault, great Grandſire I forgive thee,
Eden was loſt, as all thy Sons wou'd looſe it.
    Going towards Emmeline, *and pulling off his Gantlet.*

    Enter Philidel *running.*

  Phil. Hold, poor deluded Mortal, hold thy Hand ;
Which if thou giv'ſt, is plighted to a Feind.
For Proof, behold the Virtue of this Wand ;
Th' Infernal Paint ſhall vaniſh from her Face,
And Hell ſhall ſtand Reveal'd.
            Strikes Emmeline *with a Wand, who ſtraight*
                deſcends : Philidel *runs to the Diſcent, and*
                pulls up Grimbald, *and binds him.*

Now ſee to whoſe Embraces thou wert falling.
Behold the Maiden Modeſty of *Grimbald,*
The groſſeſt, earthieſt, uglieſt Fiend in Hell.
  Arth. Horrour ſeizes me,
To think what Headlong Ruine I have tempted.
  Phil. Haſte to thy Work ; a Noble ſtroke or two
Ends all the Charms, and diſenchants the Grove.
I'll hold thy Miſtreſs bound.
  Arth. Then here's for Earneſt ;
            Strikes twice or thrice, and the Tree falls, or ſinks :
                A Peal of Thunder immediately follows, with
                dreadful Howlings.

'Tis finiſh'd, and the Dusk that yet remains,

Is but the Native Horrour of the Wood.
But I muſt loſe no time ; the Paſs is free;
Th' unrooſted Fiends have quitted this Abode;
On yon proud Towers, before the day be done,
My glittering Banners ſhall be wav'd againſt the ſetting Sun.
(Exit Arthur.

   Phil. Come on my ſurly Slave; come ſtalk along,
And ſtamp a mad-Mans pace, and drag thy Chain.

   Grimb. I'll Champ and Foam upon't, till the blue Venom
Work upward to thy Hands, and looſe their hold.

   Phil. Know'ſt thou this powerful Wand ; 'tis lifted up;
A ſecond ſtroke wou'd ſend thee to the Centre,
Benum'd and Dead, as far as Souls can Die.

   Grim. I wou'd thou woud'ſt, to rid me of my Senſe :
I ſhall be whoop'd through Hell at my return,
Inglorious from the Miſchief I deſign'd.

   Phil. And therefore ſince thou loath'ſt Etherial Light,
The Morning Sun ſhall beat on thy black Brows;
The Breath thou draw'ſt ſhall be of upper Air,
Hoſtile to thee ; and to thy Earthy make,
So light, ſo thin, that thou ſha't Starve, for want
Of thy groſs Food, till gaſping thou ſhalt lie,
And blow it back, all Sooty to the Sky.
     Exit Philidel, *dragging* Grimbald *after him.*

G   A C T V.

ACT V.

V

Enter Ofmond *as affrighted.*

Ofm. **G** *Rimbald* made Prifoner, and my Grove deftroy'd!
Now what can fave me —— Hark the Drums and
Trumpets !   *Drums and Trumpets within.*
Arthur is marching onward to the Fort,
I have but one Recourfe, and that's to *Ofwald*;
But will he Fight for me, whom I have injur'd?
No, not for me, but for himfelf he muft ;
I'll urge him with the laft Neceffity ;
Better give up my Miftrefs than my Life.
His force is much unequal to his Rival ;
True ; ——But I'll help him with my utmoft Art,
And try t' unravel Fate.   *Exit Ofmond.*

Enter Arthur, Conon, Aurelius, Albanact, *and Soldiers.*

Con. Now there remains but this one Labour more;
And if we have the Hearts of true Born *Britains,*
The forcing of that Caftle Crowns the Day.
    Aurel. The Works are weak, the Garifon but thin,
Difpirited with frequent Overthrows,
Already wavering on their ill mann'd Walls.
    Alban. They fhift their places oft, and fculk from War,
Sure Signs of pale Defpair, and eafie Rout ;
It fhews they place their Confidence in Magick,
And when their Devils fail, their Hearts are Dead.
    Artif. Then, where you fee 'em cluft'ring moft, in Motion,
And ftaggering in their Ranks, there prefs 'em home ;
For that's a Coward heap—— How's this, a Sally ?

Enter

Enter Ofwald, Guillamar, *and Soldiers on the other fide.*

Beyond my Hopes, to meet 'em on the fquare.

Ofw. ad-⎱Brave *Britains* hold ; and thou their famous Chief
vancing.⎰Attend what *Saxon Ofwald* will propofe.
He owns your Victory ; but whether owing
To Valour, or to Fortune, that he doubts.
If *Arthur* dares afcribe it to the firft,
And fingl'd from a Crowd, will tempt a Conqueft,
This *Ofwald* Offers, let our Troops retire,
And Hand to Hand, let us decide our Strife:
This if Refus'd, bear Witnefs Earth and Heaven,
Thou fteal'ft a Crown and Miftrefs undeferv'd.

Arth. I'll not Ufurp thy Title of a Robber,
Nor will upbraid thee, that before I proffer'd
This fingle Combat, which thou didft avoid;
So glad I am, on any Terms to meet thee,
And not difcourage thy Repenting fhame;
As once *Eneas* my Fam'd Anceftor,
Betwixt the *Trojan* and *Rutilian* Bands,
Fought for a Crown, and bright *Lavinia*'s Bed,
So will I meet thee, Hand to Hand oppos'd:
My Auguring Mind, affures the fame Succefs.

To his Men. Hence out of view ; If I am Slain, or yield,
Renounce me Britains for a Recreant Knight,
And let the Saxon peacefully enjoy
His former footing in our famous Ifle.
To Ratifie thefe Terms, I fwear ——

Ofw. You need not ;
Your Honour is of Force, without your Oath.
I only add, that if I fall, or yeild,
Yours be the Crown, and *Emmeline.*

Arth. That's two Crowns.
No more ; we keep the looking Heav'ns and Sun
Too long in Expectation of our Arms.

Both Armies go clear off the Stage.

Thy

*They Fight with Spunges in their Hands, dipt in Blood;
after some equal Passes and Closeing, they appear both
Wounded : Arthur Stumbles among the Trees, Oswald
falls over him, they both Rise; Arthur Wounds him a-
gain, then Oswald Retreats. Enter Osmond from
amorg the Trees, and with his Wand, strikes Arthur's
Sword out of his Hand, and Exit. Oswald pursues
Arthur. Merlin enters, and gives Arthur his Sword,
and Exit, they close, and Arthur in the fall, disarms
Oswald.*

Arth. Confefs thy felf o'ercome, and ask thy Life.
Oswa. 'Tis not worth asking, when 'tis in thy Power.
Arth. Then take it as my Gift.
Oswa. A wretched Gift,
With lofs of Empire, Liberty, and Love.
 A Confort of Trumpets within, proclaiming Arthur's Victory,
  while they Sound, Arthur and Oswal. feem to Confer.
'Tis too much Bounty to a vanquifh'd Foe ;
Yet not enough to make me Fortunate.
 Arth. Thy Life, thy Liberty, thy Honour Safe,
Lead back thy Saxons to their Antient Elb :
I wou'd Reftore thee fruitful *Kent,* the Gift
Of *Vortigern* for *Hengift's* ill bought aid,
But that my *Britain's* brook no Foreign Power,
To Lord it in a Land, Sacred to Freedom ;
And of its Rights, Tenacious to the laft.
 Ofw. Nor more then thou haft offer'd wou'd I take.
I would Refufe all *Britain,* held in Homage ;
And own no other Mafters but the Gods.

Enter on one fide ; Merlin, Emmeline, *and* Matilda. Conon,
 Aurelius, Albanact, *with British Soldiers, bearing*
  King Arthur's *Standard difplay'd.*
 On the other fide, Guillamar *and* Ofmond, *with Saxon*
  Soldiers, dragging their Colours on the Ground.

Art. going to } At length, at length, I have thee in my Arms ;
Emm. and em- } Tho' our Malevolent Stars have ftrugled hard,
bracing her. } And hold us long afunder.   *Emm.*

Emm. We are fo fitted for each other Hearts,
That Heav'n had err'd, in making of a third,
To get betwixt, and intercept our Loves.

Ofw. Were there but this, this only fight to fee,
The price of *Britain* fhou'd not buy my ftay.

Merl. Take hence that Monfter of Ingratitude,
Him, who betray'd his Mafter, bear him hence,
And in that loathfom Dungeon plunge him deep,
Where he plung'd Noble *Ofwald.*

Ofm. That indeed is fitteft for me,
For there I fhall be near my Kindred Fiends, (*off.*
And fpare my *Grimbald*'s Pains to bear me to 'em. *Is carried*

Mer. to Arth. For this Days Palm, and for thy former Acts,
Thy *Britain* freed, and Foreign Force expell'd,
Thou, *Arthur,* haft acquir'd a future Fame,
And of three Chriftian Worthies, art the firft:
And now at once, to treat thy Sight and Soul,
Behold what Rouling Ages fhall produce:
The Wealth, the Loves, the Glories of our Ifle,
Which yet like Golden Oar, Unripe in Beds,
Expect the Warm Indulgency of Heav'n
To call 'em forth to Light——— (umphs;

To Ofw. Nor thou, brave Saxon Prince, difdain our Tri-
Britains and Saxons fhall be once one People;
One Common Tongue, one Common Faith fhall bind
Our Jarring Bands, in a perpetual Peace.

　　　　　　　Merlin *waves his Wand; the Scene changes, and*
　　　　　　　difcovers the Britifh Ocean in a Storm. Æolus
　　　　　　　in a Cloud above: Four Winds hanging, &c.

Æolus ⎱ *Ye Bluft'ring Brethren of the Skies,*
finging. ⎰*Whofe Breath has ruffl'd all the Watry Plain,*
　　　　　Retire, and let Britannia *Rife,*
　　　In Triumph o'er the Main.
　　　　Serene and Calm, and void of fear,
　　　　The Queen of Iflands muft appear :
　　　　Serene and Calm, as when the Spring
　　　　The New-Created World began,

And Birds on Boughs did softly sing,
Their Peaceful Homage paid to Man,
While Eurus did his Blasts forbear,
In favour of the Tender Year.
Retreat, Rude Winds, Retreat,
To Hollow Rocks, your Stormy Seat;
There swell your Lungs, and vainly, vainly threat.

Æolus *ascends, and the four Winds fly off. The Scene opens,
and discovers a calm Sea, to the end of the House. An*
Island *arises, to a soft Tune ;* Britannia *seated in the*
Island, *with Fishermen at her Feet*, &c. *The Tune
changes ; the Fishermen come ashore, and Dance a while ;
After which,* Pan *and a* Nereide *come on the Stage, and
sing.*

Pan *and* Nereide *Sings.*
Round thy Coasts, Fair Nymph of Britain,
   For thy Guard our Waters flow :
Proteus all his Herd admitting,
   On thy Greens to Graze below.
Foreign Lands thy Fishes Tasting,
Learn from thee Luxurious Fasting.

Song of three Parts.
For Folded Flocks, on Fruitful Plains,
The Shepherds and the Farmers Gains,
   Fair Britain all the VVorld outvyes ;
And Pan, as in Arcadia Reigns,
   VVhere Pleasure mixt with Profit lyes.

2.
Though Jasons Office was Fam'd of old,
The British VVool is growing Gold ;

No

No Mines can more of VVealth fupply:
It keeps the Peafant from the Cold,
And takes for Kings the Tyrian Dye.

The laft *Stanza* fung over again betwixt *Pan* and the *Nereide*. After which the former Dance is varied, and goes on.

Enter Comus with three Peafants, who fing the
following Song in Parts.

Com. YOur Hay it is Mow'd, & your Corn is Reap'd;
Your Barns will be full, and your Hovels
Come, my Boys, come;   (heap'd:
Come, my Boys, come;
And merrily Roar out Harveft Home;
Harveft Home,
Harveft Home;
And merrily Roar out Harveft Home.
Chorus. Come, my Boys, come, &c.

1 Man. VVe ha' cheated the Parfon, we'll cheat him agen;
For why fhou'd a Blockhead ha' One in Ten?
One in Ten,
One in Ten,
For why fhou'd a Blockhead ha' One in Ten?
Chorus. One in Ten,
One in Ten;
For why fhou'd a Blockhead ha' One in Ten?

2. For Prating fo long like a Book-learn'd Sot,
Till Pudding and Dumplin burn to Pot;
Burn to Pot;
Burn to Pot;
Till Pudding and Dumplin burn to Pot.
Chorus. Burn to Pot, &c.

3, WE'R

3.   *We'll tofs off our Ale till we canno' ftand,*
      And Hoigh for the Honour of Old England:
          Old England,
          Old England;
      And Hoigh for the Honour of Old England.
Chorus.   *Old England, &c.*

The Dance vary'd into a round Country-Dance.

Enter Venus.

Venus.   *Faireft Ifle, all Ifles Excelling,*
          Seat of Pleafures, and of Loves;
      Venus here, will chufe her Dwelling,
          And forfake her Cyprian *Groves.*

2.

      Cupid, from his Fav'rite Nation,
          Care and Envy will Remove;
      Jealoufie, that poyfons Paffion,
          And Defpair that dies for Love.

3.

      Gentle Murmurs, fweet Complaining,
          Sighs that blow the Fire of Love;
      Soft Repulfes, kind Difdaining,
          Shall be all the Pains you prove.

4

      Every Swain fhall pay his Duty,
          Grateful every Nymph fhall prove;
      And as thefe Excel in Beauty,
          Thofe fhall be Renown'd for Love.

SONG

SONG by Mr. *HOWE.*

1.

She. YOu *say, 'Tis Love Creates the Pain,*
    Of which so sadly you Complain ;
And yet wou'd fain Engage my Heart
In that uneasie cruel part :
But how, Alas ! think you, that I,
Can bear the Wound of which you die ?

2.

He. *'Tis not my Passion makes my Care,*
    But your Indiff'rence gives Despair :
The Lusty Sun begets no Spring,
Till Gentle Show'rs Assistance bring :
So Love that Scorches, and Destroys,
Till Kindness Aids, can cause no Joys.

3.

She. *Love has a Thousand Ways to please,*
    But more to rob us of our Ease :
For Wakeful Nights, and Careful Days,
Some Hours of Pleasure he repays ;
But Absence soon, or Jealous Fears,
O'erflow the Joys with Floods of Tears.

He. *By vain and senseless Forms betray'd,*
Harmless Love's th' Offender made ;
While we no other Pains endure,
Than those, that we our selves procure :
But one soft Moment makes Amends
For all the Torment that attends.

5.

Chorus of Both.

Let us love, let us love, and to Happiness haste:
Age and Wisdom come too fast :
Youth for Loving was design'd.
He alone. *I'll be constant, you be kind.*
She alone. *You be constant, I'll be kind.*
Both. *Heav'n can give no greater Blessing*
Than faithful Love, and kind Possessing.

After the Dialogue, a Warlike Consort : The Scene
opens above, and discovers the Order of the Garter.

Enter Honour, *Attended by* Hero's.

Merl. These who last enter'd, are our Valiant *Britains,*
Who shall by Sea and Land Repel our Foes.
Now look above, and in Heav'ns High Abyss,
Behold what Fame attends those future Hero's.
Honour, who leads 'em to that Steepy Height,
In her Immortal Song, shall tell the rest.

(Honour ſings.)

I.

Hon. *St.* George, *the Patron of our Iſle,*
A Soldier, and a Saint,
On that Auſpicious Order ſmile,
Which Love and Arms will plant.

2.

Our Natives not alone appear
To Court. this Martiall Prize ;
But Foreign Kings, Adopted here,
Their Crowns at Home deſpiſe.

3.

Our Soveraign High, in Aweful State,
His Honours ſhall beſtow;
And ſee his Sceptr'd Subjects wait
On his Commands below.

A full Chorus of the whole Song : After which the Grand Dance.

Arth. to Merl. Wiſely you have, whate'er will pleaſe, re-
What wou'd diſpleaſe, as wiſely have conceal'd :   (veal'd,
Triumphs of War and Peace, at full ye ſhow,
But ſwiftly turn the Pages of our Wo.
Reſt we contented with our preſent State ;
'Tis Anxious to enquire of future Fate.
That Race of Hero's is enough alone
For all unſeen Diſaſters to atone.
Let us make haſte betimes to Reap our ſhare,
And not Reſign them all the Praiſe of War.
But ſet th' Example ; and their Souls Inflame,
To Copy out their Great Forefathers Fame,

The

Spoken by Mrs. BRACEGIRDLE.

I've had to Day a Dozen Billet-Doux
From Fops, and Wits, and Cits, and Bow-ſtreet-Beaux ;
Some from Whitehal, but from the Temple more ;
A Covent-Garden Porter brought me four.
I have not yet read all : But, without feigning,
We Maids can make ſhrewd Gheſſes at your Meaning.
What if, to ſhew your Styles, I read 'em here ?
Me thinks I hear one cry, Oh Lord, forbear :
No, Madam, no ; by Heav'n, that's too ſevere. }

Well then, be ſafe———
But ſwear henceforwards to renounce all Writing,
And take this Solemn Oath of my Inditing, }
As you love Eaſe, and hate Campagnes and Fighting.
Yet, Faith, 'tis juſt to make ſome few Examples :
What if I ſhew'd you one or two for Samples ?

Pulls one out. Here's one deſires my Ladiſhip to meet
At the kind Couch above in Bridges-Street.
Oh Sharping Knave ! That wou'd have you know what,
For a Poor Sneaking Treat of Chocolat.

Pulls out another. Now, in the Name of Luck, I'll break this open,
Becauſe I Dreamt laſt Night I had a Token,
The Superſcription is exceeding pretty,
To the Deſire of all the Town and City.
Now, Gallants, you muſt know, this pretious Fop,
Is Foreman of a Haberdaſhers-Shop :
One who devoutly Cheats ; demure in Carriage ;
And Courts me to the Holy Bands of Marriage.
But with a Civil Inuendo too,
My Overplus of Love ſhall be for you.

Reads.———Madam, I ſwear your Looks are ſo Divine,
When I ſet up, your Face ſhall be my Sign :
Tho Times are hard ; to ſhew how I Adore you,
Here's my whole Heart, and half a Guinea for you.
But have a care of Beaux ; They're falſe, my Honey ;
And which is worſe, have not one Rag of Money.

See how Maliciouſly the Rogue would wrong ye ;
But I know better Things of ſome among ye.
My wiſeſt way will be to keep the Stage,
And truſt to the Good Nature of the Age ;
And he that likes the Muſick and the Play,
Shall be my Favourite Gallant to Day.

www.ingramcontent.com/pod-product-compliance
Lightning Source LLC
Chambersburg PA
CBHW031929060726

47496CB00008BA/2714